First published in hardback in Great Britain by
HarperCollins Publishers Ltd in 1992
10 9 8 7 6
First published in Picture Lions in 1993
20 19 18 17 16 15 14 13 12 11
Picture Lions is an imprint of the Children's Division,
part of HarperCollins Publishers Limited,
77-85 Fulham Palace Road,
Hammersmith, London W6 8JB
ISBN: 0 00 193618-2 (Hardback)
ISBN: 0 00 664252-7 (Picture Lions)
Copyright © Nick Butterworth 1992
The author asserts the moral right to be
identified as the author of the work.
A CIP record for this title is available
from the British Library.
Printed and bound in Singapore.

AFTER THE STORM

NICK BUTTERWORTH

Collins

An Imprint of HarperCollins*Publishers*

Percy the park-keeper couldn't sleep.
Outside his hut a great storm was
raging, with thunder and lightning and
pouring rain.

Percy wasn't frightened by the thunder
and he loved to watch the lightning as it
lit up the whole park. He didn't even
mind the rain.

But there was one thing that Percy
didn't like.

He didn't like the wind.
It blew down fences in the park and ripped branches off the trees. He didn't like it one bit.

"Oh dear," he sighed as he watched from his window. The wind tugged at the trees, making them creak and groan. "It looks like I'm going to be busy tomorrow."

He pulled his pillow over his head and tried to get to sleep.

Percy was up early in the morning. The wind had stopped and the sky was clear.

Percy loaded up his wheelbarrow with all the things he would need to make repairs and clear up after the storm. Then he set off to inspect the damage.

He felt happy as he took deep breaths of the fresh, clean air. Perhaps the damage wouldn't be too bad.

But he was wrong. Something dreadful had happened. A great big oak tree that had stood by itself on top of a little hill had been blown over by the storm.

The giant tree had been one of Percy's favourites. Now it looked very sad lying on its side with its mass of tangly roots sticking up into the air.

But it wasn't just one of Percy's favourite trees; some of Percy's animal friends lived there. Now their homes were wrecked. Percy hurried up to the fallen tree.

The animals were gathered by the tree
looking cross and unhappy. When they
saw Percy everyone started talking at once.

Percy sat down with his friends and listened as they told how the storm had brought down the great tree.

"And now we have nowhere to live," said the badger. "Some of us lived in the tree and some of us lived under it. But we're all homeless now."

Some of the rabbits looked close to tears and the fox was very sniffy. Percy passed him his handkerchief and the fox blew his nose.

Percy stood up.

"We'll just have to find you somewhere else to live," he said. "Come on everybody. Jump into my wheelbarrow." The animals felt better now that Percy was with them.

First he took them to the pine wood. But nobody wanted to live there.

"Too dark," squeaked the mice.

"Too gloomy," said the hedgehog.

So Percy took them to the shrubbery. But nobody wanted to live in the shrubbery either.

"No big trees," complained the squirrels.

"No big roots," moaned the rabbits.

"Never mind," said Percy. "We'll try across the stream."

Percy began to push the heavy
wheelbarrow over a little bridge that
crossed the stream. But as he got to the
middle of the bridge, two things happened.

Percy stumbled. And the wheelbarrow decided to see what it would be like to be a boat. SP-LASH!

Suddenly Percy and his friends found
themselves drifting downstream to
where the stream opened out into a lake.
Percy stood up and looked around.
"We'll have to paddle back to the shore,"
he said. But then something caught his eye.
"No, wait," said Percy. "Let's paddle across
to the other side of the lake. I have an idea."
The animals looked puzzled.
What was Percy up to? Slowly they
paddled the wheelbarrow across
the lake.

"Here we are!" said Percy. The squirrels jumped ashore and tied up the wheelbarrow to the roots of an enormous hollow tree that grew by the water's edge.

"Now this is my plan," said Percy. Everyone gathered round as Percy explained his idea.

"Is everybody clear?" Everyone nodded. "Then let's get to work!"

They began by unloading all Percy's tools and the planks of wood from the wheelbarrow. Then Percy explained exactly what he wanted each one to do.

He showed the badger how to use a saw and he showed the squirrels how to knock in nails. The fox drilled holes and the rabbits screwed in screws. The mice were kept busy fetching and carrying for everyone else.

At lunchtime they took a short break to share some of Percy's peanut butter sandwiches. Then they got busy again.

At long last their work was finished.
A very tired Percy stood back to
admire their handiwork.

Now the squirrels had
a brand new home. . .

and so did the mice.

The rabbits had
a new home. . .

and so did the badger.

And the fox.

And the hedgehog.

In fact, every one of Percy's friends
had a fine new place to live.

"Well done everybody!" said Percy. "This is the best tree house I've ever seen!"

"What about you Percy?" called the badger. "Aren't you going to join us?"

Percy smiled.

"I think I'll stick to my old hut," he said.

"Besides," said Percy, taking an acorn out of his pocket, "I still have one job left to do back at the little hill!"